THE JOKER AND HARLEY QUINN'S JUSTICE LEAGUE JAILHOUSE

BY
LOUISE SIMONSON

ILLUSTRATED BY
TIM LEVINS

STONE ARCH BOOKS
a capstone imprint

Published by Stone Arch Books in 2018
A Capstone Imprint
1710 Roe Crest Drive
North Mankato, Minnesota 56003
www.mycapstone.com

STAR39623

Cataloging-in-Publication Data is available
at the Library of Congress website.
ISBN: 978-1-4965-5980-7 (library binding)
ISBN: 978-1-4965-5987-6 (paperback)
ISBN: 978-1-4965-5999-9 (eBook PDF)

Summary: With the help of a nefarious billionaire, the Joker
and Harley Quinn hatch a plan to lock up the Justice League
for good. Can the world's greatest super heroes thwart the
Joker and Harley before it's too late? Or will this perilous
pair doom the heroes forever in a Justice League jailhouse?

Editor: Christopher Harbo
Designer: Bob Lentz

Printed in the United States of America.
010825S18

CONTENTS

When the champions of Earth came together to battle a threat too big for a single hero, they realized the value of strength in numbers. Together they formed an unstoppable team, dedicated to defending the planet from the forces of evil. They are the . . .

{ ROLL CALL }

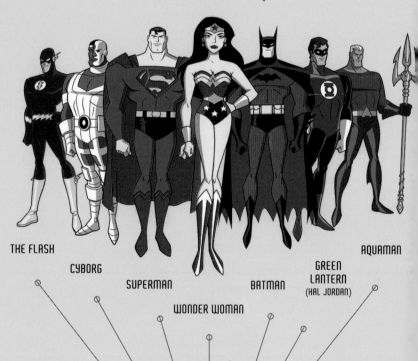

THE FLASH

CYBORG

SUPERMAN

WONDER WOMAN

BATMAN

GREEN
LANTERN
(HAL JORDAN)

AQUAMAN

MARTIAN
MANHUNTER

HAWKGIRL

HAWKMAN

GREEN ARROW

BLACK CANARY

THE ATOM

SUPERGIRL

RED TORNADO

POWER GIRL

GREEN LANTERN
(JOHN STEWART)

SHAZAM

PLASTIC MAN

BOOSTER GOLD

BLUE BEETLE

ZATANNA

VIXEN

METAMORPHO

ETRIGAN
THE DEMON

FIRESTORM

HUNTRESS

CHAPTER 1

THE CRAZY KIDNAPPING

Superman soared toward the Watchtower, the Justice League's headquarters. The huge satellite hung in orbit above North America. Its monitors told the heroes what was happening on Earth and in space.

The Man of Steel entered the space lock and jabbed the close button. The door snapped shut. As he waited impatiently for the chamber to carry him to the meeting room, he scanned the satellite with his super senses. *I wonder why the Justice League asked me to report so quickly,* he thought.

Superman's X-ray vision showed him Batman, Wonder Woman, Green Lantern, and Cyborg waiting in the command center. His super-hearing let him listen to their distant conversation.

Wonder Woman turned from the room's wall of windows to face the others.

"Superman's here," she said. "But The Flash and Huntress haven't arrived. Batman, you said Huntress called this meeting. What is it about?"

Superman raised an eyebrow. *Interesting,* he thought. *Wonder Woman doesn't know any more than I do.*

Batman sighed. "Huntress heard an odd rumor that the Joker has hatched a bizarre scheme that somehow involves the Justice League. She said she'll tell us what she knows when she arrives."

"So where is she?" Wonder Woman asked.

"I was wondering the same thing," Superman said as he stepped from the elevator. "There was trouble in Metropolis, and I'm running late. I thought I'd be the last to arrive."

Cyborg frowned. "I talked to her a while ago. She was aboard one of our cargo planes, waiting for The Flash. They should have been here by now."

Green Lantern shrugged. "It's probably nothing to worry about. Still, we could give them a call to make sure they're okay."

* * *

The Flash raced through the streets of Central City. Its buildings seemed to blur as he dashed toward the small private airport where Huntress was waiting for him.

It was a day with one emergency after another. Bank robberies, jewelry heists, and mad scientists had kept The Flash running all day. He had been so busy he hadn't had time to stop, much less eat. Moving at super-speed used a lot of energy. If he didn't keep fueled, he'd slow down and eventually fall over.

So, even though he was late, he'd stopped at Tonio's, his favorite pizza joint. Juggling the pizza box as he ate on the run had slowed him down a bit, but it had been worth it. He could feel his energy returning. He hoped Huntress wouldn't be too mad at him for being late.

As the Scarlet Speedster bit into his seventh slice, the airport came into sight. *I'll offer Huntress the last piece,* he thought. *No way she'll be mad at me after that.*

The Flash knew Huntress would be waiting inside a Justice League cargo plane. The hangar that housed it was right beyond the small control tower.

"I'm still hungry," The Flash muttered as he rounded the corner. "I could really use some dessert!"

And suddenly, there it was before him — a huge creamy chocolate pie.

"What — !?" he cried. Then **SPLOPP!** He ran right into it.

The Flash froze. He couldn't move. He couldn't speak. He gasped for air — and hit the ground hard.

* * *

The Joker and Harley Quinn stared down at The Flash's unconscious body.

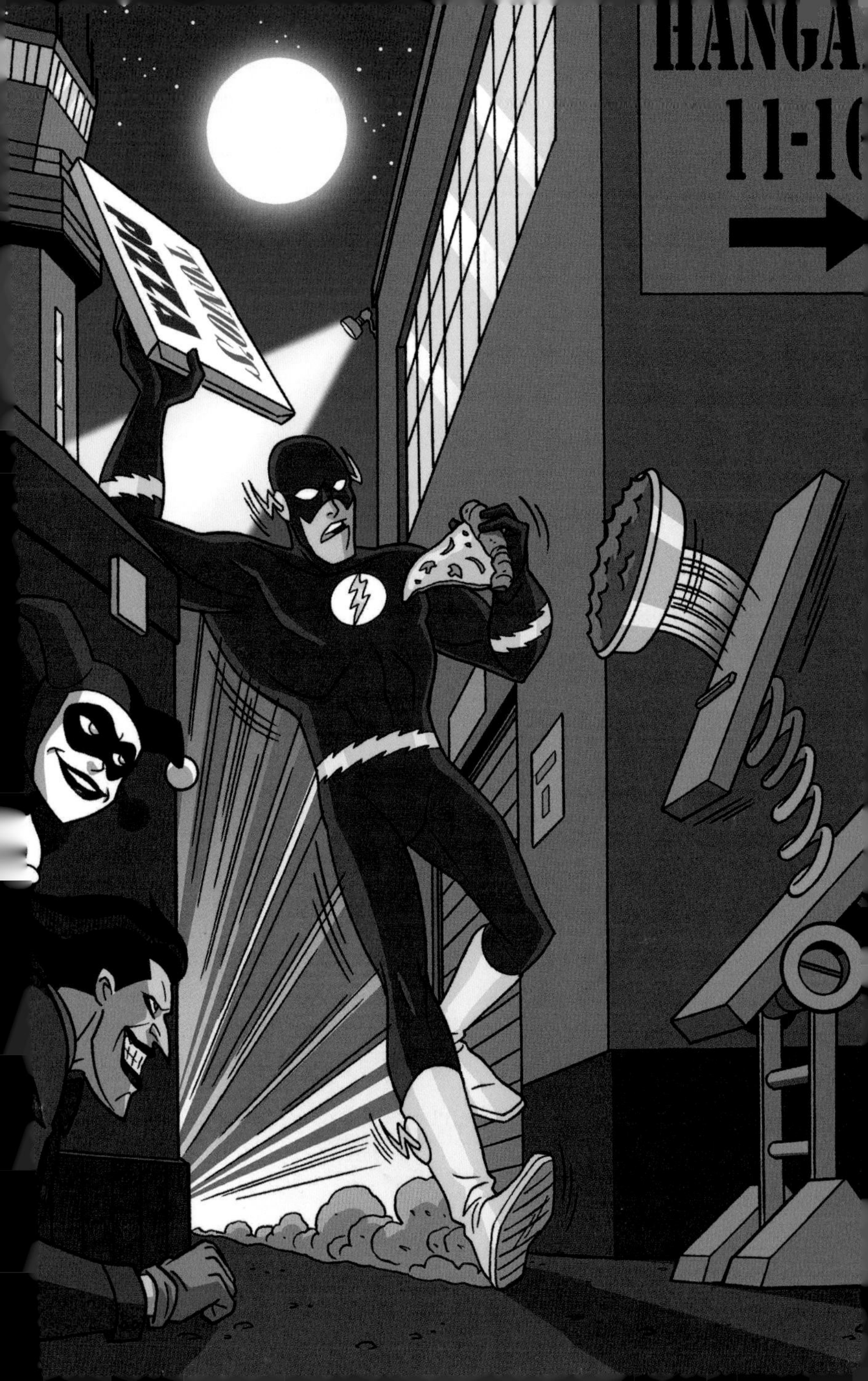
HANGA
11-1

"Why is he just lying there?" Harley poked him with the head of her giant mallet. Then she bent over, studying The Flash's whipped cream covered face.

"Paralyzing agent," the Joker replied, chuckling to himself. "It's my own special formula. Collect the speedster, will you? I have to call Lex."

Harley slung The Flash over her shoulder, grateful for her enhanced strength. The Joker turned his back on her and punched a number into his cell phone.

Lex Luthor appeared on the view screen. "You have them?" he growled.

The Joker shrugged. "I have one of them."

"Superman?" Lex asked eagerly.

"The Flash," the Joker said. "He'll serve as bait to lure the others."

"Don't bother me with details! You know why I'm paying for this operation," Lex growled. "I want Superman! Let me know when you have him. You can do what you want with the rest of the Justice League, but Superman is mine."

Harley wrinkled her nose as Lex clicked off. "Rude," she muttered. "I don't like him."

The Joker raised an eyebrow. "I don't like him either, but he's our supplier of dirty tricks. For now he's a necessary evil."

Harley sighed. "I guess." Then she looked more cheerful. "I do love your plan to trap the Justice League in Arkham Asylum. So clever. It will show them just how it feels to be in jail there!"

The Joker winked at her. "There is one tiny, but tantalizing, tweak to that plan," he said. "In the end, they will all die laughing."

Harley whirled around to look at him. "All of them? Even Superman? Lex won't like that."

"Lex can lump it —" the Joker snarled. "Shhhh! Someone's coming!"

The Joker dragged her around the edge of the building. Harley put down The Flash and peeked around the corner.

"It's Huntress! She's not a regular member of the Justice League," she whispered. "What is she doing here?"

Huntress stood outside of the hangar. "I don't see The Flash," she said, speaking into her communicator. "Hold on, Batman. I'll take a look around the airport."

She walked past the building Harley and the Joker hid behind. Then she stopped as she spotted something on the ground.

"A Tonio's pizza box!" Huntress said into the communicator. "The Flash must have been here. There's a half-eaten slice on the ground. And what looks like a pie tin and some weird foam —"

Harley stuck out her mallet. Huntress tripped over the handle. She fell forward and her hand slammed into the gooey pie tin.

"Yuck!" she said, then collapsed in a heap.

Harley grinned. "I guess there are a lot of Justice League wannabes! But your knockout foam worked on her too! This must be our lucky day!"

The Joker reached down and clicked off the hero's communicator. Then he tossed it aside. "Still, the one we really want is Superman. Especially Superman! He's the most powerful. Without him, the others will fall —"

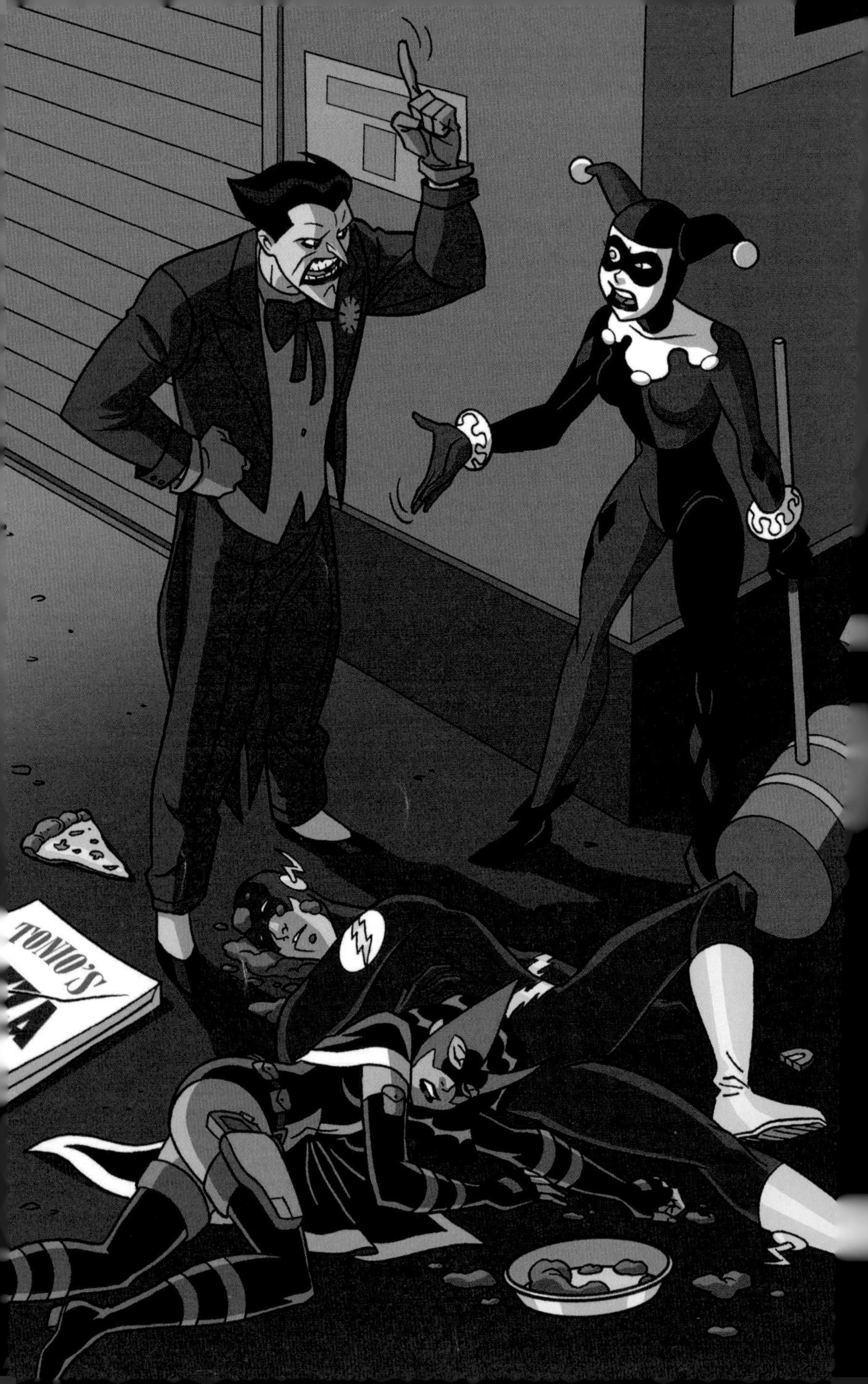
TONIO'S

"They'll still have Wonder Woman," said Harley, dragging The Flash out beside Huntress. "She's more powerful than he is."

"Get real! Superman's the most powerful!" the Joker said, grinning evilly. "Except for the Kryptonite thing."

Harley folded her arms. "Wrong! Wonder Woman can do everything Superman can!"

"She doesn't have X-ray vision," the Joker reminded her.

"Superman can't see through lead!" Harley countered.

The Joker shrugged. "A minor weakness we'll use to our advantage. But does she have X-ray vision? Or heat vision?"

Harley got mad now. "No. But she doesn't fall over when she gets near Kryptonite either! She has no weaknesses. Not one!"

"Every Justice Leaguer has a weakness!" the Joker said. "And I am prepared to take advantage of all of them. Now come along, and bring those two with you!"

Harley sighed. She flung The Flash over her shoulder and lifted Huntress under one arm. "You're *my* weakness," Harley muttered behind the Joker's back. "And you know it!"

"What did you say?" the Joker asked, not bothering to turn around.

Harley rolled her eyes. "I said — What about the pizza box? And the pie tin?"

"Leave them," the Joker replied. He reached over, tore a white ball from the back of her costume's collar, and tossed it onto ground beside the other junk.

"Hey!" Harley scowled at him. "Why did you do that?"

"In case they send someone who is exceptionally dim."

"But —" Harley trudged behind him, lugging the two heavy heroes. "But they'll just tell Batman, and *he'll* know exactly what it means."

The Joker grinned back at her. "I know. I'm counting on it."

*   *   *

Batman glanced up from his handheld communicator, an eyebrow raised in concern. Superman, Wonder Woman, Green Lantern, and Cyborg frowned back, puzzled and alarmed. They had all heard Huntress speak, then a loud **WHAKK!**, and an indistinct voice saying, "This must be our lucky day!"

Then the communicator had gone dead.

It was obvious what had happened.

"Someone attacked The Flash and has now attacked Huntress," Batman said. "We need to go to Central City and find out what's going on."

Batman, a brilliant detective, was the obvious choice to make that journey. But Superman and Wonder Woman insisted on going with him. If there was danger, the three of them would be an effective force against it.

They decided that Green Lantern and Cyborg would remain on the Watchtower monitoring Earth.

"We'll call you the minute we know what's going on," Batman said grimly.

"If you need our help, we'll be there," Green Lantern said.

Within minutes Batman, Wonder Woman, and Superman entered the vast hangar where the Javelin, the Justice League's spacecraft, rested. Not all of the Justice League members could fly through space unaided. The Javelin was there to shuttle them from Earth to the Watchtower and back again.

This time though, Superman planned to fly to Earth in the Javelin with his friends. They had a lot to talk about.

"So?" he asked Batman as the plane rose off the hanger floor and soared out into space. "What do you think is going on?"

CHAPTER 2

LAUGH OR LOSE

The Joker steered the small LexCorp submarine through the murky Gotham River. As it skimmed along the bottom, its headlights glinted off the rusted cars and boats, discarded tires, and other trash stuck deep in the mud.

Harley frowned out the window. "Why are people such slobs?" she muttered. She whirled to face The Flash and Huntress, who were tied up and unconscious behind them. "If those heroes want to do something good, why don't they clean up the river instead of bothering innocent villains like us?"

The Joker flashed a snide grin. "Since you think Wonder Woman is so great, why don't you ask her?"

Harley scowled over at him. "I will once we've captured her." Then she smiled at him crookedly. "So . . . what is her weakness, anyway? Does she *really* have one?"

The Joker raised an eyebrow. "Have you ever known me to be wrong?"

Harley opened her mouth — she could think of several times he had been very wrong — but shut it again. Around the Joker, it was best to keep your opinions to yourself.

Out the sub window, the granite rock beneath Arkham Asylum came into view. Harley knew the prison had been founded hundreds of years ago. Although its ancient core had expanded over time, the facility still rested on the original stone foundation.

The sub's headlights revealed a circular hole lined with bricks. In her excitement, Harley squealed. "Is that it? The tunnel you found? Mr. J, you are the cleverest!"

"Aren't I, though?" the Joker said as he guided the sub through the opening and into a passage beyond. He had discovered this secret passageway during one of his many escapes from Arkham. He'd been waiting for the perfect time to use it.

The submarine surfaced in a small cavern and pulled up to a crumbling brick dock.

"Are you going to tell Lex we're here?" Harley asked as she shoved open the hatch.

The Joker shrugged. "He's leaving the details to me." He brushed past Harley and clambered onto the dock. He glanced back at her. "Still — get The Flash and Huntress out of there while I send a text."

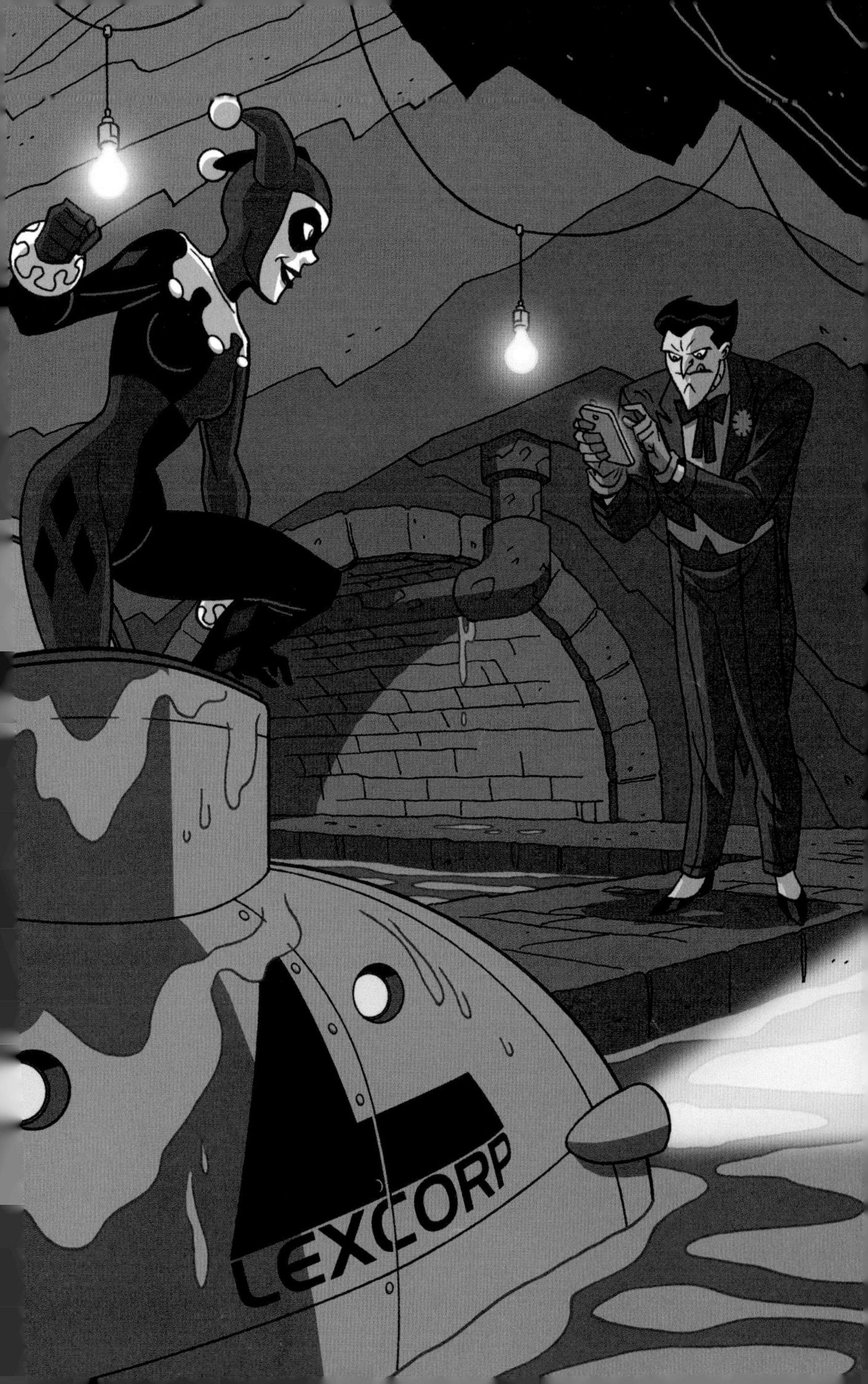
LEXCORP

Beneath the curved ceiling of the tunnel, the Joker stalked ahead, muttering as he typed his text: "Arrived at Arkham. JL will follow clues I left. Be fun to see who stumbles into my trap next."

Slinging the unconscious Flash over her shoulder and dragging Huntress by her cape, Harley stalked down the winding tunnel after him. The Joker seemed to think lugging fallen heroes was all she was good for. "If we don't know who's coming, how can we know what kind of trap to set?" she grumbled.

The Joker waved his hand airily. "Don't worry. Between my brain and Luthor's bankroll, everything has been planned for."

The Joker stopped before a circular wooden door. Looking back at Harley, he threw it open with a flourish. "Welcome to our newest secret lair!" he said.

Burdened with one hero and dragging the other, Harley trudged through the opening. She felt sulky and unappreciated.

But when Harley got inside, she looked around. The room had originally been an ordinary circular cavern. But the Joker had transformed it into something far more interesting.

Electric cables snaked across the floor. Thirteen large flat screens were mounted in a circle to the ceiling. And facing each screen was a giant playing card resting on a small metal platform. The cards ranged from the Ace to the King of Hearts, and each one had shackles fastened to its upper corners. In the center of the room, a polka-dot tarp covered something large and lumpy.

Strangest of all, the walls and floor had been completely lined with lead.

"Wow!" Harley cooed. "Mr. J, this time you have outdone yourself!" It was hard to stay mad at her Puddin' when he did something so fascinating. "What now?" she asked eagerly.

"Now tie our guests to the cards facing the screens," the Joker said.

Harley picked up The Flash and carried him toward the King card.

"No!" the Joker snapped. "He gets the Jack! The King of Hearts is reserved for Superman."

Harley lugged the unconscious hero toward the Jack. Together she and the Joker fastened the shackles around his wrists.

"Then the Queen card must be for Wonder Woman," Harley said. "And the Ace is for Batman?"

"Bingo!" the Joker said. "I'm saving the highest cards for the Justice League's main members. But I've included a few extras for any tagalong heroes they bring."

Harley shrugged. "Like Huntress! Justice League wannabes!"

The Joker grinned. "Exactly. Though I doubt they see themselves like that. Huntress gets the Eight."

Harley frowned. "I don't think plain old shackles will hold these two for long."

The Joker laughed. "There's nothing plain about them."

Huntress's eyes were opening. The Flash was testing his bonds and glaring at them. "Where am I?" he asked.

The Joker rubbed his hands. "Now the real fun begins! An introduction, if you please!"

Harley rolled her eyes, but then stepped forward. "Preeeesenting . . . the Clown Prince of Crime, that Wizard of Wit, the Genius of Gagsters, the One and Only . . . the JOKER!"

The Joker stood beneath the ring of screens before the bound heroes. "For your entertainment, a selection of images — my favorite moments from my maddest, baddest, funniest capers will soon begin. In case you miss the jokes, my voice-over will explain my comic brilliance."

The Joker snapped his fingers, and the screens lit up with the title: THE JOKER'S GREATEST HITS.

Images flashed across the screens.

Harley giggled and clapped her hands as a picture of a pile of fish wearing bright red Joker smiles appeared. "The Joker Fish! One of my favorites!"

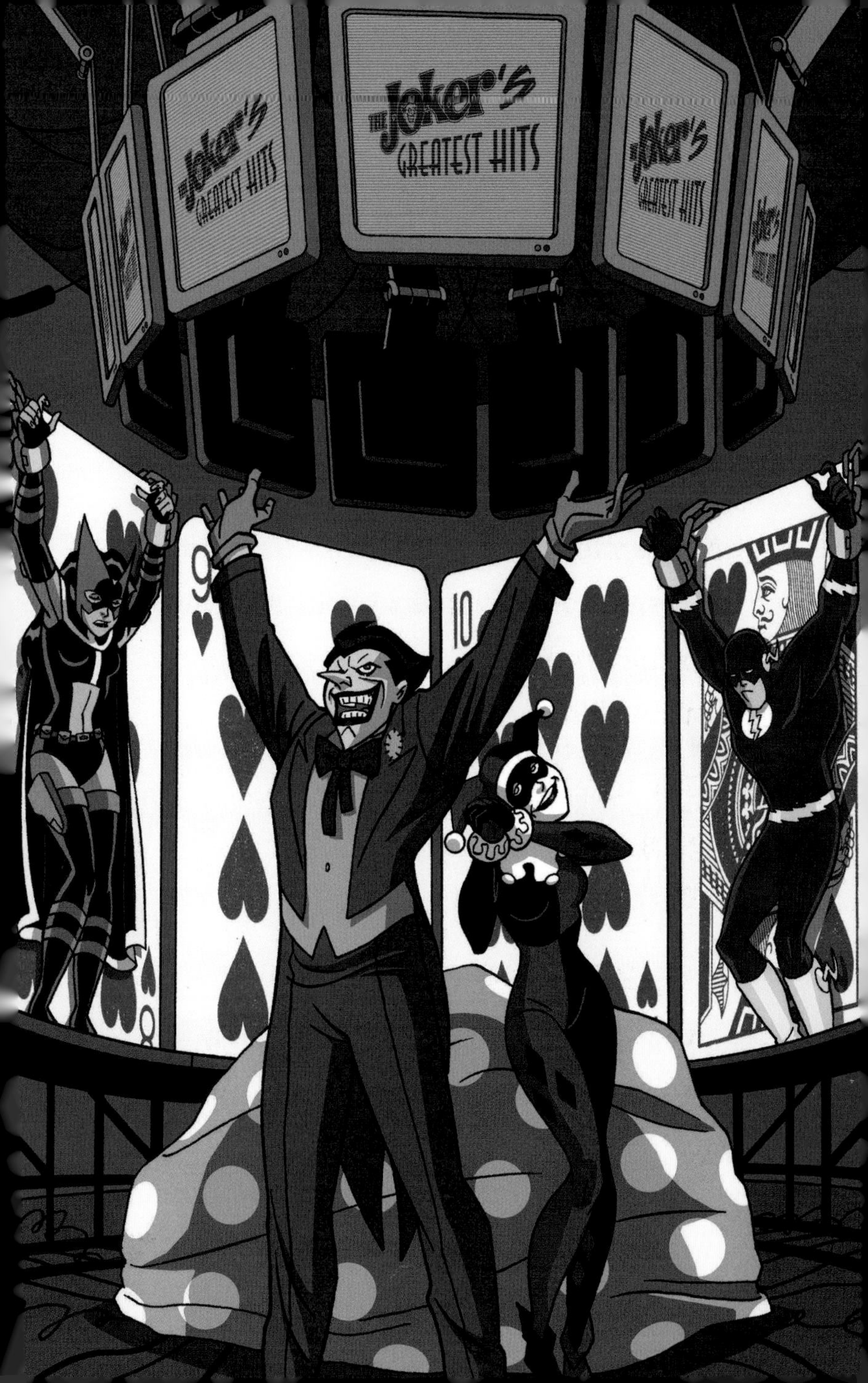
THE Joker's GREATEST HITS

But The Flash and Huntress just stared at the screens, stone-faced.

"I see you don't yet get the joke. But you will. To prove it, I expect you to laugh — nonstop." The Joker stalked to the center of the room and jerked aside the polka-dot tarp. Beneath it was a huge pile of dynamite. "Your cards are wired to these explosives. Stop laughing and — KA-BOOM!"

"We'll escape," The Flash said.

"I know how sneaky you heroes can be," the Joker jeered. "So I have taken extra precautions. Your own bonds have been modified to prevent your vibrating through them. In addition, you are standing on metal platforms. Those platforms are switches wired to the explosives. As long as they're pressed down by your weight, you're safe. But move off the switch and — good-bye Arkham!

"The Justice League will come for us," Huntress murmured.

The Joker grinned. "I'm counting on it! And now, I suggest you laugh. The previews are over. The show is about to begin."

*   *   *

The Javelin neared the small private airport outside of Central City just after sunset. Batman settled the craft with a vertical landing, and the heroes looked around. The control tower was dark at this hour, the airport deserted.

SWISH! The cockpit flipped open. Wonder Woman and Superman flew into the air, then landed on the tarmac while Batman leaped down after them.

"Looks like nobody's home," the Man of Steel said.

Batman stalked toward the hangar that housed the Justice League cargo jet. He tugged at the door, but it was locked.

"Want me to open it?" Wonder Woman asked, flexing her fingers.

Batman grinned over at her. "You mean wrench it off its hinges? Not necessary. I have my lock picks." He patted his Utility Belt. "But I doubt we'll find what we're looking for in there. Huntress was attacked outside."

Wonder Woman smiled at him. "Then, by all means, let's start our search for clues outside."

Superman and Wonder Woman rose into the air, senses alert.

Hovering above the control tower, they scanned the dark ground far below. But Superman saw what lay there clearly.

He was the first to spot the odd assortment of articles lying on the ground, to one side of the control tower. His telescopic vision showed him the details.

"I've found something," he called to Batman and Wonder Woman. "A Tonio's box and a half-eaten slice of pizza."

Superman landed beside the box as Wonder Woman kneeled to retrieve something else. "A communicator and — what's that?" She frowned as she reached for a circular tin smeared with globs of foam.

"Don't touch it!" Batman snapped.

"Why?" Wonder Woman asked, pulling her hand back.

"It's a pie plate. We won't know what that foam contains until I analyze it. But I know where it came from."

Superman frowned. "Where?"

"The Joker!" Batman said. "The old pie-in-the-face trick is a classic."

"The Joker wasn't alone," Wonder Woman said. She scooped up a little white ball and raised an eyebrow.

"Harley Quinn!" Batman said. "They took The Flash and Huntress and left these clues on purpose."

"The Joker wants us to come after him?" Wonder Woman said.

Superman smiled grimly. "And where would he go but Gotham City?"

CHAPTER 3

THE ARKHAM ANGLE

Superman flew over Gotham City. Far below, the streets and alleys were blanketed by fog. But Superman could still see figures moving like ghosts through the mist.

Rather than wait for Batman to refuel the Javelin, Superman had flown ahead at super-speed. He was sure his super-vision and super-hearing were their best hope of locating their friends.

And they needed to find The Flash and Huntress quickly. The Joker was mad. The more time he had to develop his schemes, the more dangerous he became.

As he searched the sinister darkness, Superman felt a tug of longing for his own gleaming Metropolis. Even after midnight *his* city pulsed with neon lights and hectic energy. He knew its heartbeat, could tell almost by instinct if something wasn't right. Here in Gotham City, he felt less sure.

The Man of Steel flew on, searching, but his efforts were constantly interrupted. A car accident. A bank robbery. A power plant explosion. People needed his help, and he just couldn't ignore them.

Superman stopped suddenly. He hovered above the tall spire of Gotham Cathedral, listening intently. For an instant he thought he had heard The Flash's laughter — a faint *HA! HA! HA!* It sounded fake and oddly strained, but it was definitely from The Flash. Where was it coming from?

Superman followed the sound to an area along the Gotham River — an area that held the infamous Arkham Asylum.

The Flash's hoarse laughter ended in a sudden cough.

I've lost him, Superman thought.

Then the sound was taken up by a woman's voice. A higher pitched *HEE! HEE! HEE!* rang in his ears.

Huntress, Superman thought. *It has to be her. What is going on?*

He hovered above Arkham, searching the prison with X-ray vision. His gaze traveled past the main gate and into the sprawling complex made up of buildings. Within them he saw high-tech cells housing mad and dangerous criminals. He saw guards. A hospital area. A kitchen. Nothing unusual.

Superman sharpened his focus, looking deeper. The buildings rested on a deep stone foundation. Below was a basement. And finally a sub-basement that must have been blasted from bedrock when Arkham was built long ago.

Within that sub-basement was a room that was a complete blank. "Lined in lead," Superman murmured. "The one substance I can't see through, and a great way to get my attention." Someone as clever as the Joker really should have known better.

Superman hovered above the river, studying the sub-basement structure with his X-ray vision. An access tunnel ran beneath Arkham Asylum, past the lead-lined room, straight to the Gotham River. The passage looked old, as if it hadn't been used in years.

Until very recently.

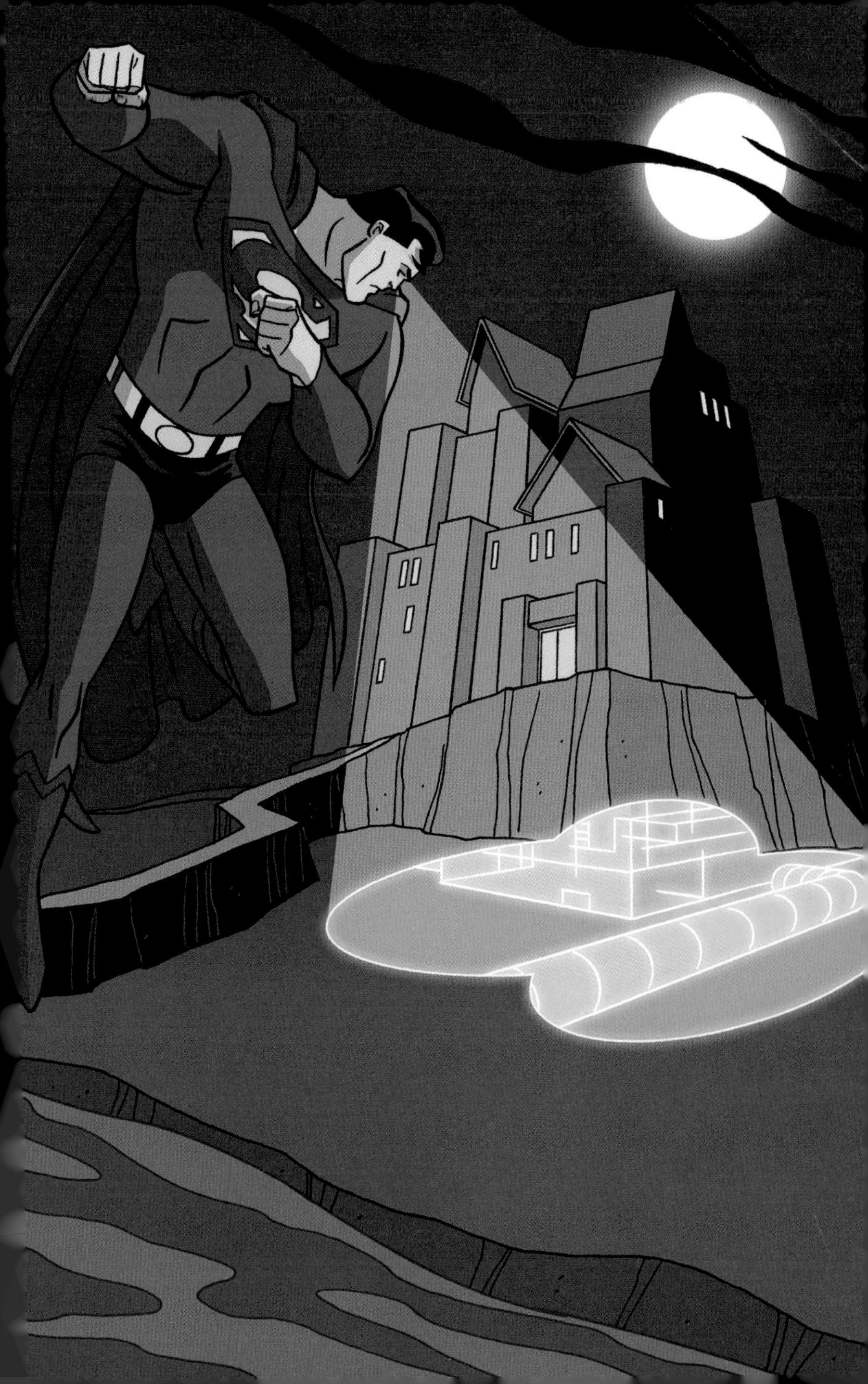

Batman and Wonder Woman won't be here for a while, the Man of Steel thought. *I still have time to check it out.*

Superman dropped like a stone into the water. With powerful strokes, he swam through the current toward the hidden tunnel entrance.

He ducked through a brick-lined hole, then surfaced in a stone cavern half filled with river water. He flew into the air, water dripping from his cape, and landed on a crumbling dock beside a small LexCorp submarine.

Does this mean Lex is involved in this? Superman wondered. Everything Lex did was for his own personal gain. So what did he expect to gain from the Joker's scheme?

The Man of Steel shrugged. He'd find out soon enough.

Superman followed the sounds of laughter through the twisting tunnel. As he neared the lead-lined room, the sounds became more distinct. The false laughter — The Flash was laughing again now — overlaid an announcer's voice describing how the Joker had stolen a nuclear warhead. Superman remembered that incident and frowned. *How could The Flash possibly think that event was funny?* he thought.

A loud **CRACK!** came from the ceiling. Superman looked up, startled. Green dust fell around him. He staggered, dizzy, suddenly feeling very ill.

What's wrong with me? he thought.

Superman collapsed to his knees, no longer able to stand. He suddenly knew what was wrong. How Lex Luthor was involved. What his enemy hoped to achieve.

Lex wants me, he thought. Then he toppled unconscious onto the stone floor.

* * *

The Joker rubbed his hands gleefully as he stared down at Superman's body.

"I knew he wouldn't be able to resist a lead-lined room. So very predictable." The Clown Prince of Crime sighed with mock pity. "Such impressive strengths. And just a few tiny tragic flaws!"

Harley glared at him suspiciously. "Where did you get Kryptonite?"

"Three guesses." The Joker grinned. "Lex does have his uses."

"So — I guess you'll call him right away to tell him you have Superman?" she asked. The Joker looked shocked.

"And give him an excuse to pull his financing?" he cried. "Hand him the prize of my growing collection? Are you mad?"

"Clinically speaking, Mr. J, we both are," Harley said with a laugh. "I'm a professional, so I know these things." She had been a psychiatrist — the Joker's psychiatrist — before she joined him in his life of crime.

Harley tugged on Superman's cape, but he was hard to budge. Besides having superpowers, the Man of Steel was also super-dense. This time it took both Harley and the Joker to haul the prize prisoner to the Joker's Greatest Hits Room.

"Superman really is . . . the most powerful," the Joker puffed as they heaved the unconscious hero through the door. "And yet . . . you saw . . . how easily . . . I captured him."

"And you think that makes you even more powerful than he is?" Harley asked as they dragged Superman toward the King of Hearts card. "Maybe, but I bet capturing Wonder Woman isn't going to be so easy."

* * *

The Javelin hovered above a landing pad in a remote area outside Gotham City. Slowly, it settled to the ground.

The cockpit flipped open and Wonder Woman flew out, dragging a camouflage tarp after her. She waited until Batman had leaped to the ground, then she dragged the tarp over the spacecraft.

Once it was hidden, she followed Batman into the Batcave. She landed next to his workstation, with its bank of computers. "You've rebuilt your computers again?"

Batman smiled. "I merely added a few components. I have to keep up with the times, and the additional computing power comes in handy."

"I bet. Gotham City's a big, complicated city." Wonder Woman frowned. "I wonder if Superman found anything. Shouldn't he have checked in by now?"

She reached for her communicator, tapped a few buttons, and then put it to her ear. She waited a moment. Then she frowned at the screen. "No answer. Not even a beep. There's just . . . nothing."

"I thought I heard you arrive, sir," a voice interrupted.

Wonder Woman smiled up at the butler, dressed in a robe and slippers. He came down the stairs that led from the mansion high above. "Alfred, how nice to see you again!"

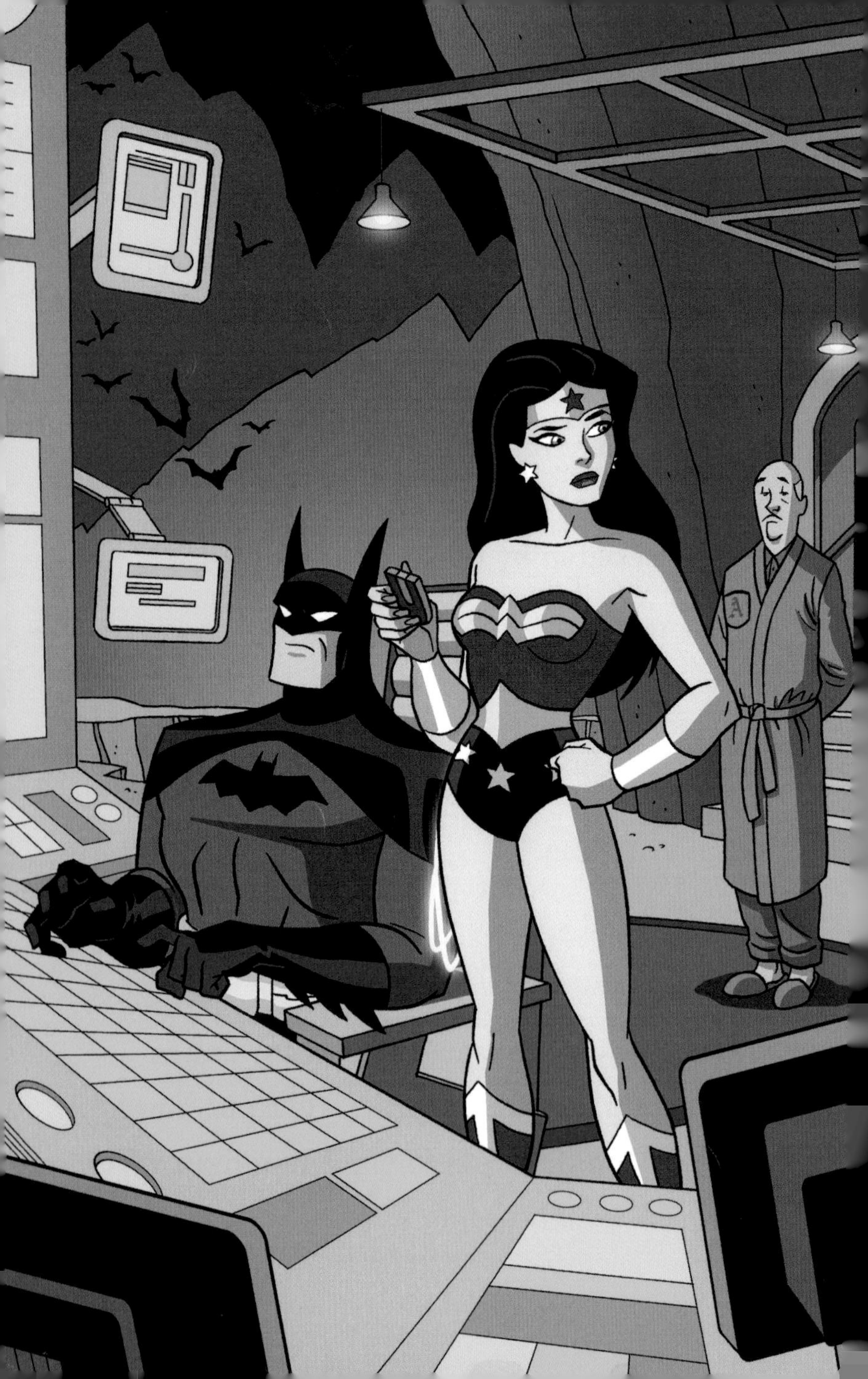

"A pleasure to see you as well, Wonder Woman," Alfred said. "But I hear the worry in your voice, and I agree. Something has happened. The TV news was filled with tales of Superman sightings above Gotham City until about an hour ago. It seems some night fishermen saw him disappear into the Gotham River near Arkham. There's been no word of him since."

Wonder Woman bit her lip. "It looks like the Joker wants to destroy the Justice League, Alfred. He captured The Flash and Huntress. If he's managed to capture Superman, he must have been planning this for a long time." She glanced at Batman. "I think it's about time we called the others."

CHAPTER 4

WEAK OR WILY

"Thanks, Alfred," Batman said, noticing the butler yawn widely. "It's late. You've done all you can for now. I'll contact you if I need further help."

"Please do." Alfred smiled grimly. Then, stifling another yawn, he climbed the stairs that led up to the mansion. He knew Green Lantern and Cyborg would be in Gotham City soon. With the Justice League on the job, he didn't have to worry.

"We need to do some research while we wait," Batman said.

Wonder Woman sighed. She was a woman of action. Studying data on a computer had little appeal. But instead of arguing, she plopped down before a screen and asked grumpily, "What kind of research?"

Batman didn't have real superpowers like she and Superman did. What he did have was the power of his mind. His extraordinary intellect gave him an almost superhuman ability to find clues and see patterns. This had made him the world's foremost detective and the terror of Gotham City's criminals.

Batman's fingers flew over the keyboard. "Superman dove into the Gotham River near Arkham," he said. "Whatever he was after couldn't be reached from above. If we study the river as it flows past Arkham, and the architecture of Arkham itself, we may be able to figure out where he went."

Wonder Woman frowned. "And your new computers will help?"

Batman smiled grimly. "That's the plan."

Working together, Batman and Wonder Woman studied the river and land on which Arkham Asylum was built. They searched historic records and the old building plans dating back to the late eighteenth century.

Finally, they found an old article from a long vanished newspaper. It had a passing mention of an ancient natural tunnel deep in the bedrock beneath Arkham Asylum.

Wonder Woman leaped to her feet. She was excited now. "That's what Superman was looking for — what he found. But he was captured somehow. The Joker was ready for him, like he was ready for The Flash and Huntress. He thinks he's so clever. But we can use that overconfidence against him."

"What do you mean?" Batman asked.

"The Joker's captives can't escape, or they would have already," Wonder Woman said. "Since he's holding Superman, he's probably keeping him weak with Kryptonite. What else could accomplish that? And he probably just can't wait to capture more of us."

Wonder Woman paused, then smiled. "So . . . I think I should enter the tunnel to find and rescue them," she said.

"By yourself?" Batman raised a skeptical eyebrow. "Superman tried and failed. What makes you think you'll succeed?"

"Superman has more abilities than I do, but I don't have his weakness," she said. "Kryptonite doesn't affect me."

Batman rubbed his chin. "And if the Joker captures you anyway?"

Wonder Woman shrugged. "I'm pretty invulnerable. He can't hurt me. But there *are* all these crazy rumors. If he thinks he can capture me, I'll let him — for a while. It's one way to find out what we're up against."

"How will we find you?" Batman asked.

Wonder Woman grinned broadly. "I'll be wearing a hidden communicator and a GPS tracker. It will lead you, Green Lantern, and Cyborg directly to his hideout."

*　*　*

The eastern sky grew brighter as Wonder Woman soared over Arkham Asylum. She compared the building to the blueprints she and Batman had studied. The new hospital building rested directly above the tunnel. Facing it, Wonder Woman held her breath and dropped into the icy river.

The water seemed very, very dark. For a moment she envied Superman's ability to see in wavelengths beyond those of humans. Then her eyes slowly adjusted, and she noticed a faint glimmer of light coming from the bedrock.

Wonder Woman swam toward it and there it was — the entrance to the tunnel she and Batman had discovered. She arrowed though the small opening and surfaced in a dimly lit cavern.

Rubbing water from her eyes, Wonder Woman looked around. The natural cavern she was in looked like the Batcave, but it was half full of water. A string of lights hung on the wall, throwing reflections on the water. More lights led into the winding tunnel. That all figured. But the LexCorp submarine docked nearby was unexpected.

Wonder Woman flew out of the water, landed on the dock, and wrung water from her hair. Then, with a grin, she carefully felt behind her tiara as she straightened it. *Good,* she thought. *The tiny communicator linking me to the Justice League is still hidden there.*

Looking around the creepy cavern, Wonder Woman was suddenly glad that Batman could track her movements.

"Just as we thought," she murmured. "A tunnel and a cave . . . and, surprise! A LexCorp sub! I guess the Joker and Harley aren't in this alone."

Wonder Woman headed into the tunnel, following tracks in the dust. She found dry scuff marks, likely made by the Joker or Harley dragging something. And on top of them were Superman's footprints — still damp from river water.

Looking behind her, Wonder Woman saw a wet trail of her own footprints as well. *Why walk when I can fly?* she thought. She rose in the air and shot down the tunnel. *If I move fast enough, I just might surprise them!*

But as she neared a corner, Wonder Woman heard a loud **WHOOSH!** A blast of strange smelling air surrounded her. *So much for surprise,* she thought as she landed. *They knew I was coming.*

The Joker stepped out from the shadows. Harley slid up behind him. Both villains were wearing clear plastic rebreather masks. That meant they had used some kind of poisonous gas on her.

"Well, well, well. Just look who we caught this time — your invulnerable hero Wonder Woman!" The Joker laughed wickedly. "Not so invulnerable now, is she?"

"Ummm . . . I dunno," Harley muttered. She glanced at Wonder Woman nervously. "Shouldn't she be rolling around on the floor laughing?"

"Don't be ridiculous," the Joker said. "I didn't use laughing gas. Luthor gave me fear gas that he got from the Scarecrow. It paralyzes its victims with fear. Absolutely guaranteed!"

"She doesn't look scared to me." Harley smirked. "Maybe you can get your money back, Mr. J."

"I probably didn't use enough," the Joker muttered angrily. "I better hit her with another blast!"

WHOOSH!

The second blast was stronger — and much smellier.

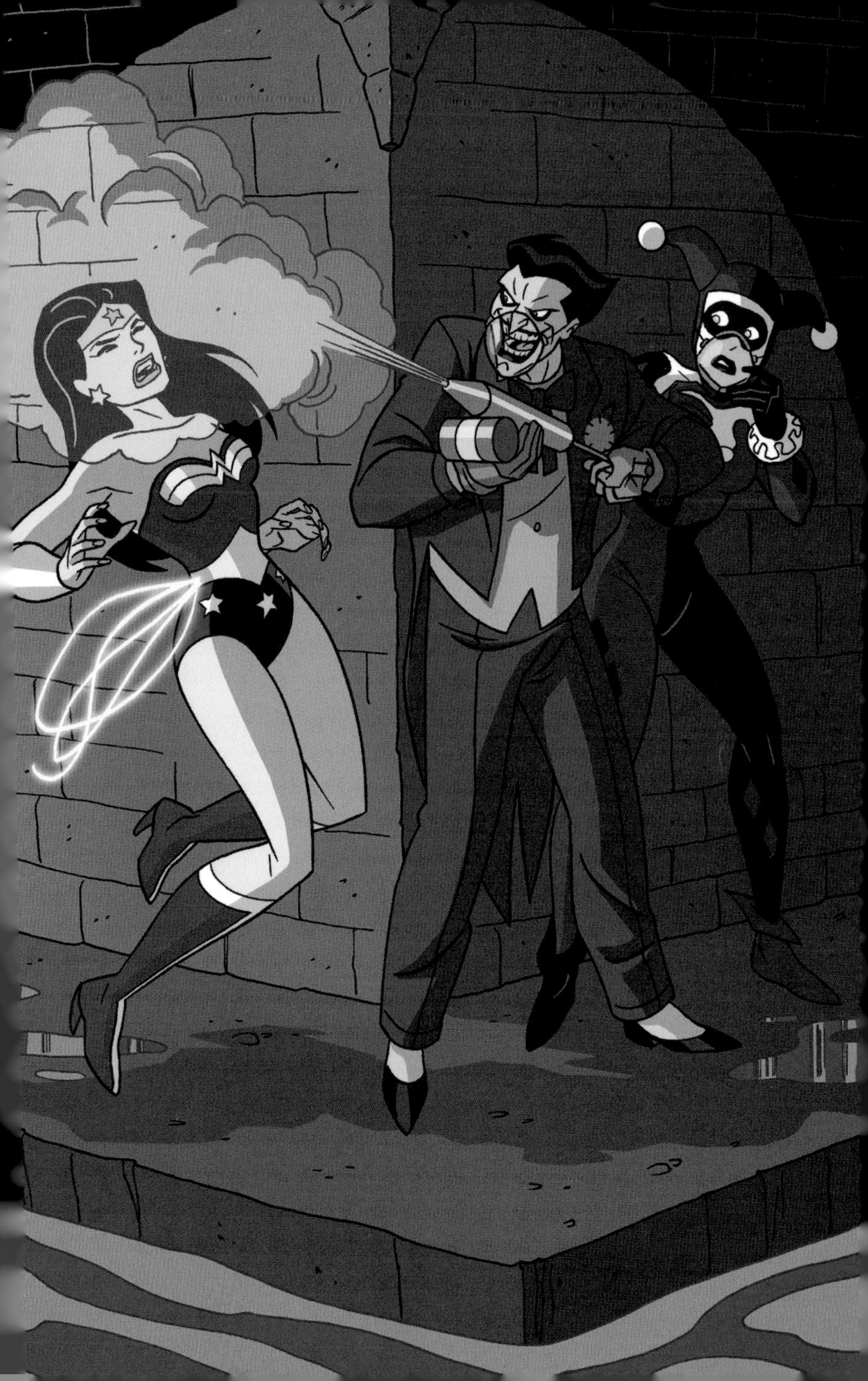

This time Wonder Woman knew how the Joker expected her to react. For a moment she considered knocking the villains' heads together. But the Justice League needed to know what the Joker was up to and how Luthor was involved. That meant keeping the Joker talking.

Wonder Woman fell to the ground and pretended to freeze with terror.

"No weaknesses? *Ha!*" Joker gloated. "Just look at her! She was easier to capture than Superman! Bring her along to the Greatest Hits Room," the Joker said.

"I thought she'd do better than that," Harley muttered as she hefted Wonder Woman over her shoulder. The Amazon was so tall her long, dark hair almost dragged on the floor. Harley almost tripped over it as she carried Wonder Woman to the secret lair.

"Amazons are supposed to be super tough! So what happened?" Harley muttered as she propped Wonder Woman against the Queen of Hearts card.

You'll find out soon enough, Wonder Woman thought. She cracked one eye open. What was all that noise and strained laughter anyway?

She quickly scanned the room and saw they were in a cavern lined with lead. The Flash, Huntress, and Superman were shackled to giant playing cards. Each one faced a noisy screen showing a different video of the Joker's maddest capers. Superman had a chunk of green rock tied around his neck.

And there's the Kryptonite, Wonder Woman thought. *Superman can't escape on his own, but what about the others? And why are they all laughing?*

Harley scowled over at the Joker. "What happens when the fear gas wears off? Wonder Woman has super-strength!"

"Not a problem!" The Joker snatched the golden lasso from Wonder Woman's belt. Instead of shackling her, he wrapped the rope around her, tying her to the huge card. "Luthor told me she can't escape if you bind her with her own lasso."

"And you believe him because . . . why?" Harley sneered. The Joker's gloating smugness was starting to make her mad.

"Because he doesn't know I already have Superman," the Joker said. "Until he gets his prize, he won't double-cross me."

Wonder Woman opened her eyes and glared at the Joker. "You obviously don't know Lex Luthor very well," she said.

Wonder Woman was almost ready to quit pretending. But first she wanted answers. "You won't get away with this," she said.

"Of course I will!" The Joker flashed his toothy smile. "Now here are the rules."

The Joker quickly explained his trap. If any of the captives stopped laughing or stepped off the metal switches, the explosives would detonate. Then they, Arkham, and much of Gotham City would be destroyed.

When the Joker finished, Harley giggled. "Quite the brilliant trap Mr. J's come up with, isn't it?"

It was, Wonder Woman realized. In fact, it was diabolical. She could see that The Flash and Huntress were exhausted. They hadn't eaten or slept since arriving here. And, poisoned as he was, Superman could barely force out a hollow *HA! HA! HA!*

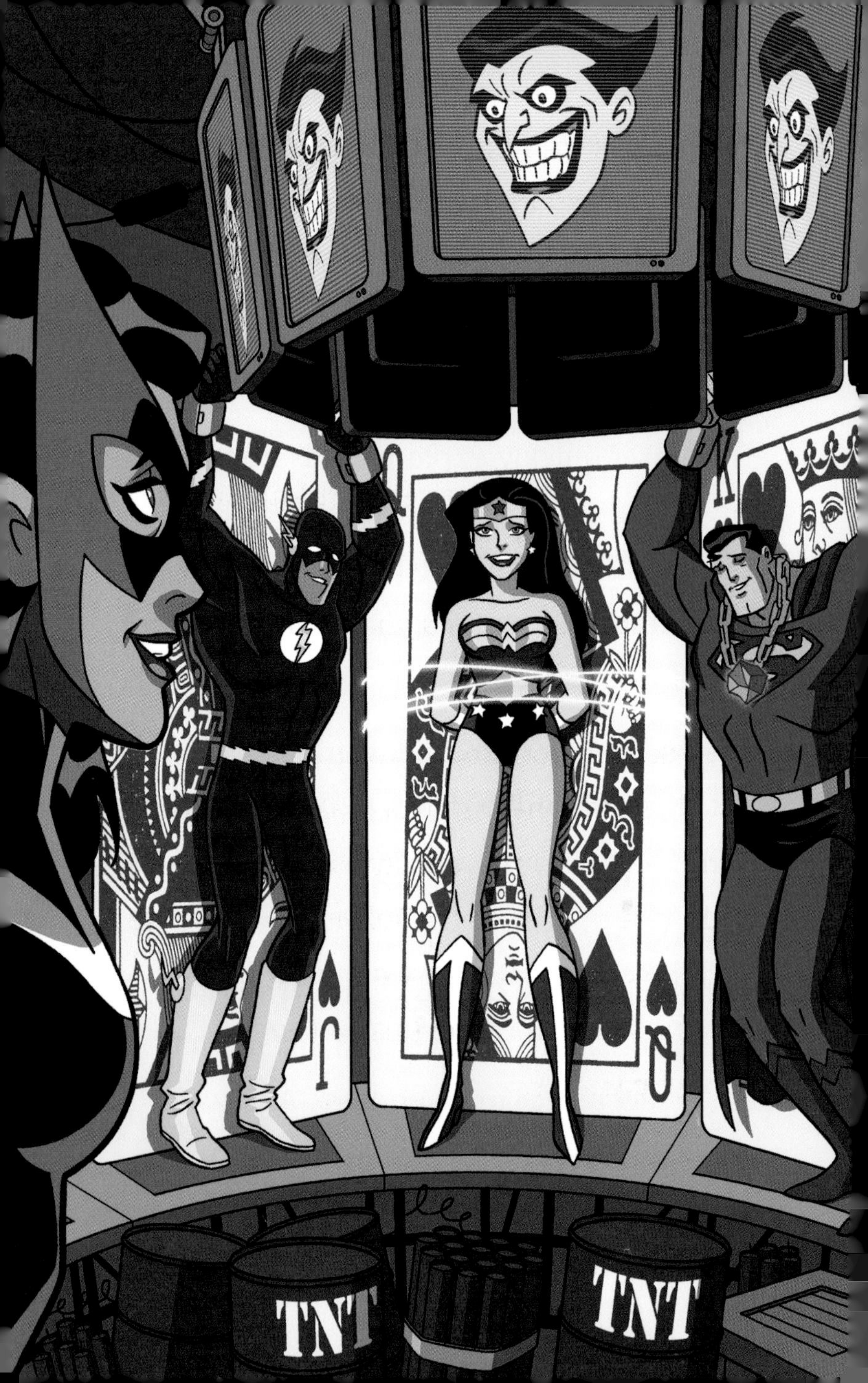
TNT
TNT

The screen in front of Wonder Woman flickered to life. The Joker's grinning face popped into view and cackled with evil laughter. Then images of his past attack on the Justice League's Watchtower satellite began to play.

"Three . . . two . . . one! Start laughing!" the Joker said.

The Amazon warrior sighed. *What else can I do*, she thought.

Wonder Woman had no way to save them all, not by herself. Not without putting Arkham Asylum and the city in danger. She would have to remain the Joker's captive. She hoped the communicator was still working. She hoped the rest of the Justice League would arrive soon.

Then she laughed.

CHAPTER 5
THE LAST LAUGH

It was close to sunrise when Batman, Green Lantern, and Cyborg plunged into the Gotham River. Unlike Wonder Woman and Superman, they remained dry by traveling comfortably inside of a glowing green bubble created by Green Lantern's power ring.

Lit by the emerald glow, they spotted the tunnel entrance easily. Green Lantern stretched out the bubble's shape as they swept through the passage. They bobbed to the surface inside the cavern and floated onto the dock beside the LexCorp submarine.

"The Joker knew Wonder Woman was here," Batman murmured. "He was waiting for her."

"I hear you," Cyborg said. He stopped at the tunnel entrance, studying the dimly lit passage. His mechanical senses registered the pulses of tiny LexCorp cameras carefully hidden in the ceiling.

"Hidden cameras," Cyborg muttered. He signaled the others to stay back. Then he fired his pulse cannon, which instantly disabled any electronics within range.

"I took out the cameras," Cyborg said as he scanned farther down the tunnel. "I'm surprised Superman didn't see them."

"He probably didn't care if the Joker knew he was coming," Green Lantern said. "That clown's whole plan is really disturbing."

"Even for a madman," Batman agreed. "But thanks to Wonder Woman, we know about the danger to the city."

Cyborg walked ahead, scanning with his sensors. Finally, he nodded toward a circular door set into the wall.

"They're in there," Cyborg murmured. "The infamous Greatest Hits Room we heard so much about."

The heroes could clearly hear the noise coming from the room. It sounded like a jumble of the Joker narrating his adventures mixed with hoarse, fake laughter.

"Ready?" Batman asked. They had made a plan based on what Wonder Woman had discovered. But they wouldn't be sure it would work until they got inside.

Cyborg nodded.

"One . . . two . . . three . . . ," Green Lantern said. His ring projected a giant emerald hammer. **WHAM!** It smashed into the door. **BAM!** The door to the Greatest Hits Room flew open!

Harley gaped at the three heroes standing there. The Joker's eyes bulged.

The villain whirled on his captives. "You think you're saved, but you're not! Whatever you do, don't move from those switches! And don't stop laughing! Or BOOM will be the last sound we all hear!"

"HA! HA! HA!" Wonder Woman laughed for real this time. She didn't dare move from the switch she was standing on — not yet. But she shrugged off her bindings, looped up her lasso, and hooked it onto her belt. She knew that Batman had a plan. When the time came, she would be ready.

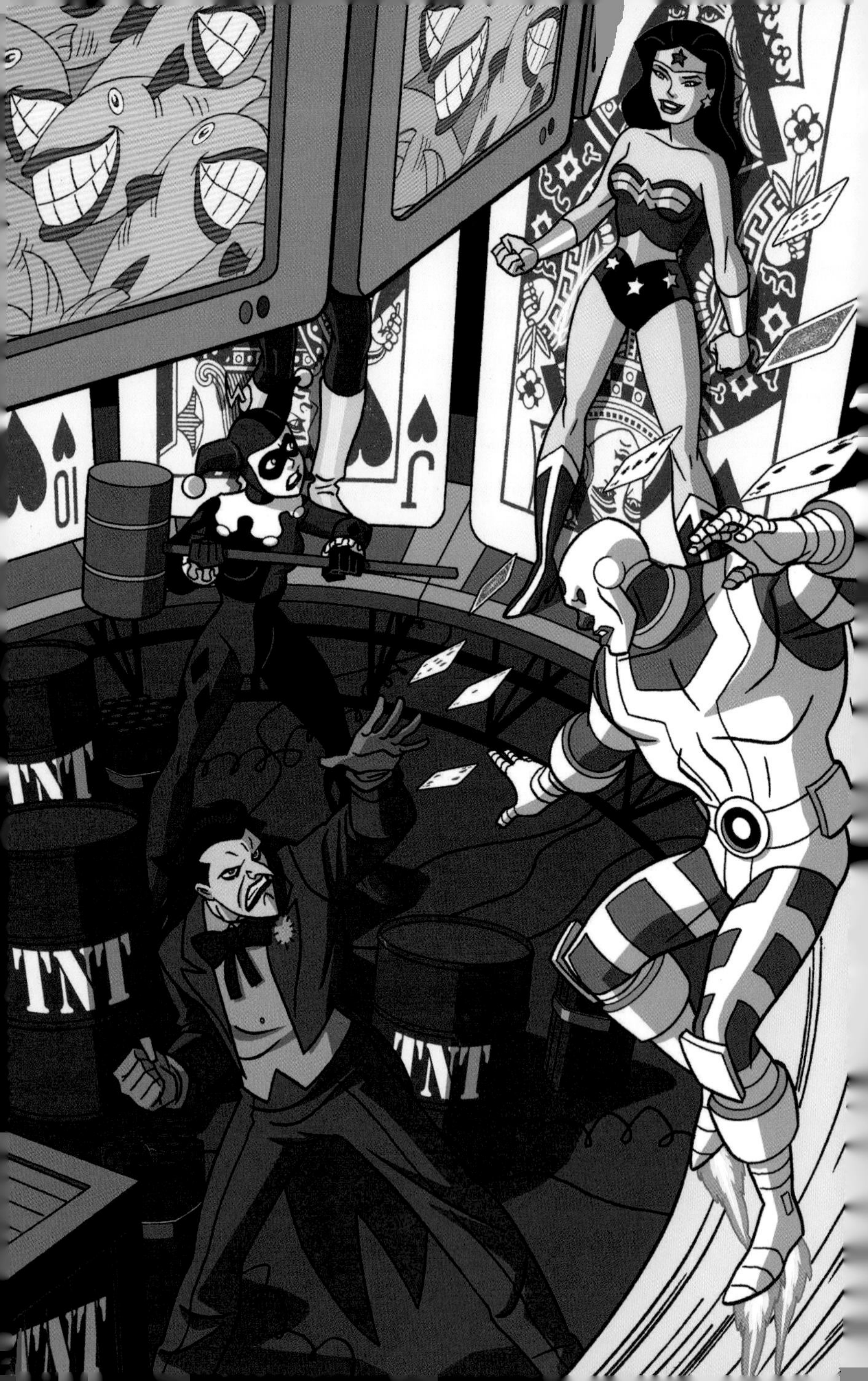
TNT
TNT
TNT
TNT

Harley noticed and whirled on her. "You were faking it! Your lasso doesn't keep you bound!" She squinted her eyes. "I bet the Scarecrow's poison gas —"

"No effect — HA! HA! — at all," Wonder Woman replied, resuming her fake laughter. "But I needed to get in here HA! HA! to find out what you were up to. HA! HA!"

Cyborg activated the jets in his feet and blasted toward the Joker.

"Focus, Harley," the Joker shouted. He pulled razor-sharp cards from his pocket and hurled them at Cyborg. The hero easily knocked them aside with his metal arm and kept on coming.

"Focus! Right!" Harley snatched up her mallet. As Cyborg tackled the Joker, she slammed it down hard on his back.

KLANGG! It hit metal, but bounced off leaving Cyborg completely unharmed. So she slammed him again!

While Cyborg fought Harley and the Joker, Batman pulled lock picks from his Utility Belt. He rushed to free Huntress, and then he unshackled The Flash.

"Stay there and keep laughing," he said. "The safety of the city depends on it!"

The Flash rolled his eyes. "Not to — HA! HA! — mention — HA! HA! — our safety!"

"No kidding! HA! HA!" said Huntress. "This is — HA! HA! — the weirdest mission I've — HA! HA! — ever been on!"

Only Superman remained. Batman lifted the Kryptonite from around his neck, shoved it into a lead-lined compartment in his Utility Belt, and unlocked Superman's shackles.

No longer held upright, Superman fell onto the switch plate. Kryptonite poisoning had left him too weak to stand, though he still forced out a weak, "HA! HA! HA!"

"Superman is fading fast," Batman said to Wonder Woman. "We'll have to get him into the sunlight."

Wonder Woman knew Superman got his energy from the sun. Only the rays of the sun could restore him. "I'll — HA! HA! — get him there!" she said. "Just say the word."

Batman glanced around. The heroes had been freed. Cyborg held the squirming, angry Joker by the collar. Harley was clutched beneath Cyborg's arm. Superman, weak as he was, had stumbled to his feet and stood on his switch, upright but swaying.

It was time to put the trickiest part of the plan into action.

Green Lantern stepped forward. He used his ring's energy to create glowing emerald images of The Flash, Huntress, Superman, and Wonder Woman. They floated in the air above the real heroes' heads.

"As I lower these doppelgängers onto the switches, step off slowly," he said. "If I can maintain the exact pressure of your weight, it should fool the switches and buy us time to disconnect the explosives. Just keep laughing."

Slowly, Green Lantern lowered The Flash's doppelgänger. The Flash slid off his switch. It stayed depressed.

Nothing exploded.

The plan seemed to be working.

Next came Huntress.

And then Superman.

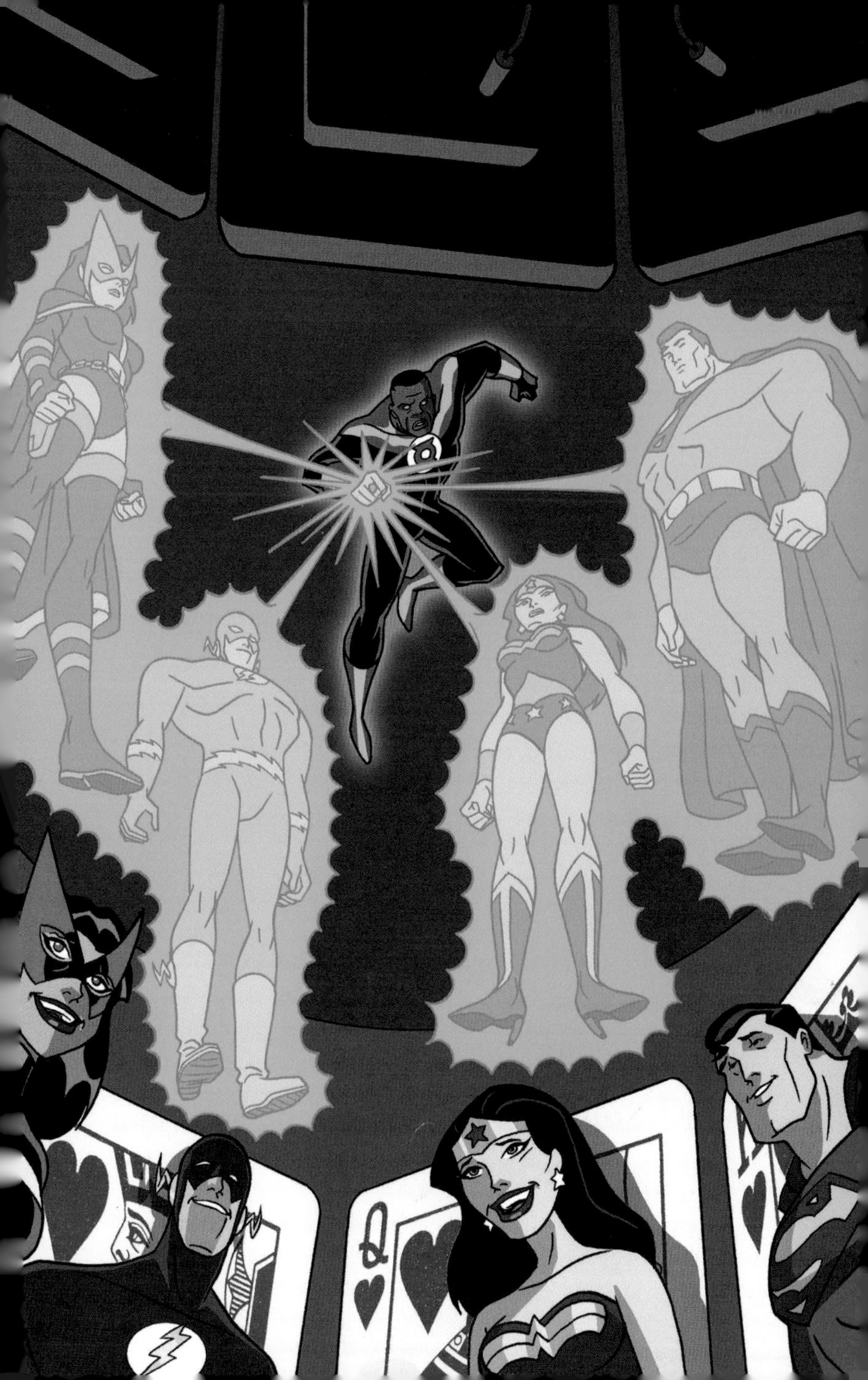

But before the duplicate Superman touched the switch, the weakened hero stumbled off. The sensitive switch popped up — and a loud alarm began to wail.

"Run!" the Joker shouted at Cyborg. "Get me out of here!"

Recorded images of the Joker's face, huge and smiling, appeared on the screens. "Looks like it's curtains for you — and for Gotham!"

Then the Joker's recorded voice began a countdown: "Five . . . four . . . three . . ."

"Go!" Green Lantern yelled. "Now! Use your super-speed! I'll handle Plan B!"

Cyborg, carrying the Joker and Harley, jetted from the chamber. The Flash grabbed Huntress and zipped after him. Wonder Woman snatched up Batman and Superman and flew down the tunnel.

Looking back, Wonder Woman could see Green Lantern standing there, concentrating. He used his ring's power to create a bubble construct around the deadly explosives piled in the center of the cavern.

When she reached the water-filled cavern, Wonder Woman heard a muffled **BA·BROOHM!** It shook the floor and rattled the cave walls. But the cave didn't collapse. Arkham Asylum was still intact. The city had been saved.

"Green Lantern!" she shouted.

"I'm fine," he answered. "One of the walls blew out, though. Come and see what I've found behind it."

Wonder Woman put Batman down on the dock. "I'll be right back," she said. "Now hold your breath," she told Superman as she dropped with him into the cavern's waters.

Wonder Woman swam through the passage, out into the river, and soared up into bright sunlight.

The morning sun struck Superman full on his face. Wonder Woman could almost see the energy and life flooding back into him.

"Are you okay?" she asked.

"I'm fine. Now. Thanks to your help," Superman said, with a wry smile. "I hate Kryptonite."

"I don't blame you," Wonder Woman said. "You know where the Joker got it?"

"I know," he said grimly. Then, with a wave, he flew east at super-speed.

Wonder Woman smiled. She didn't need to guess where he was heading.

* * *

When Wonder Woman returned to the cavern, she found Green Lantern peering through a hole blasted in the wall. He had discovered the Joker's control room. Cyborg had plugged his hardware into the bank of computers. He had learned all the technical details of the Joker's plan.

Now the Justice League was ready to witness the conclusion of this crazy scheme.

Batman shoved the Joker in front of the video screen. Cyborg dialed up Lex Luthor.

Luthor's face appeared on the screen. "It's about time you checked in, Joker," he snarled. "Did you capture Superman?"

Before the Joker could answer, a deep voice behind Luthor said, "Not exactly."

And Superman's hand came down hard on Lex's shoulder.

* * *

It was a short flight back to prison, but Harley and the Joker bickered all the way.

"I told you Wonder Woman didn't have any weaknesses!" Harley said. "But did you believe me? Nooo!"

"She has a weakness!" the Joker snarled. "She cares about people. She risked her life to get information that would foil my plan and save the city!"

Harley frowned. "That's not a weakness, Mr. J! I'd risk my life for you, and you'd risk yours for me!"

"Would I?" the Joker said, glancing away from her.

"Of course you would," Harley answered. "You're my sweet Puddin', after all!"

The Justice League watched as guards marched the Joker and Harley to separate cells in Arkham Asylum.

"So much for the weaknesses of others," The Flash said. "The Joker's weakness is he thinks he's the cleverest guy in the room. But guess what? This last caper, like the others, belongs on a blooper reel."

"Yeah," agreed Huntress. "The Joker's Greatest Flops."

⟨ END ⟩

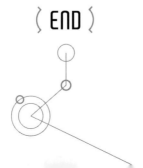

JL DATABASE: VILLAINS

THE JOKER AND HARLEY QUINN

The Joker and Harley Quinn first met in Arkham Asylum. The Joker, an evil madman transformed by a vat of toxic waste, was in lockup. Harley, known then as Dr. Harleen Quinzel, was a psychiatrist at the prison. When the Joker told Harley the heartbreaking, yet fake, story of his troubled childhood, she fell in love and helped him escape. Now Harley Quinn and the Joker clown around Gotham City. They are two of Batman's most dangerous enemies and a thorn in the side of the Justice League as well.

LEX LUTHOR

THE JOKER

CHEETAH

SINESTRO

CAPTAIN COLD

BLACK MANTA

AMAZO

GORILLA GRODD

STAR SAPPHIRE

BRAINIAC

DARKSEID

HARLEY QUINN

BIZARRO

THE SHADE

MONGUL

POISON IVY

MR. FREEZE

COPPERHEAD

ULTRA-
HUMANITE

CAPTAIN
BOOMERANG

SOLOMON GRUNDY

BLACK ADAM

DEADSHOT

CIRCE

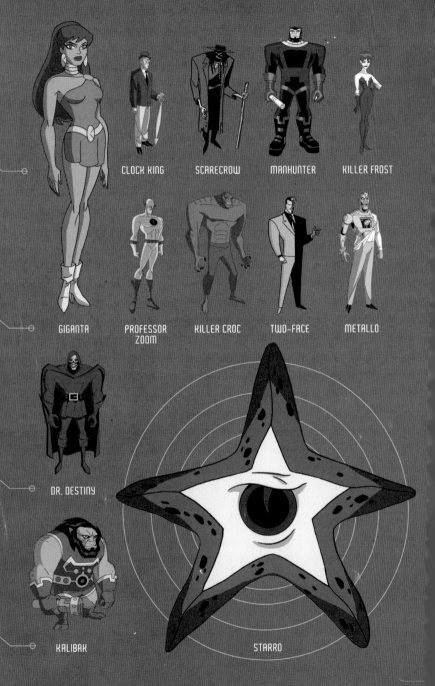

CLOCK KING

SCARECROW

MANHUNTER

KILLER FROST

GIGANTA

PROFESSOR
ZOOM

KILLER CROC

TWO-FACE

METALLO

DR. DESTINY

KALIBAK

STARRO

STRENGTH IN NUMBERS

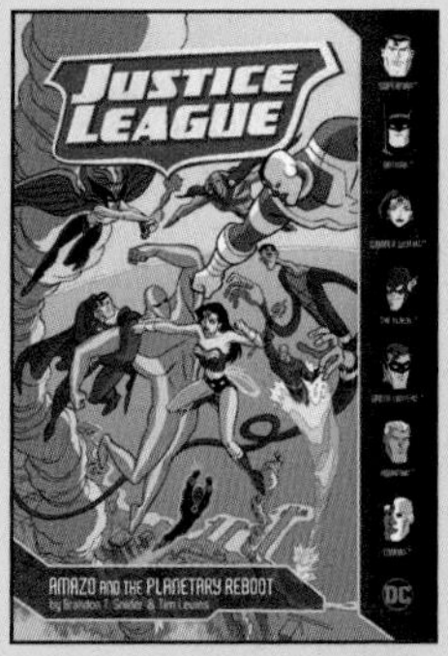
JUSTICE LEAGUE
AMAZO AND THE PLANETARY REBOOT
by Brandon T. Snider & Tim Levins
DC

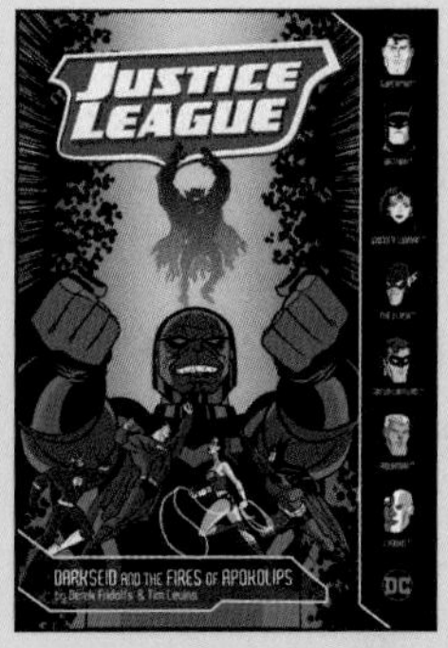
JUSTICE LEAGUE
DARKSEID AND THE FIRES OF APOKOLIPS
by Derek Fridolfs & Tim Levins
DC

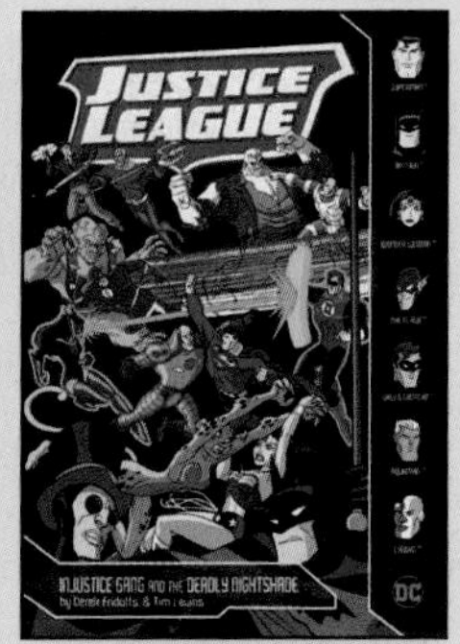
JUSTICE LEAGUE
INJUSTICE GANG AND THE DEADLY NIGHTSHADE
by Derek Fridolfs & Tim Levins
DC

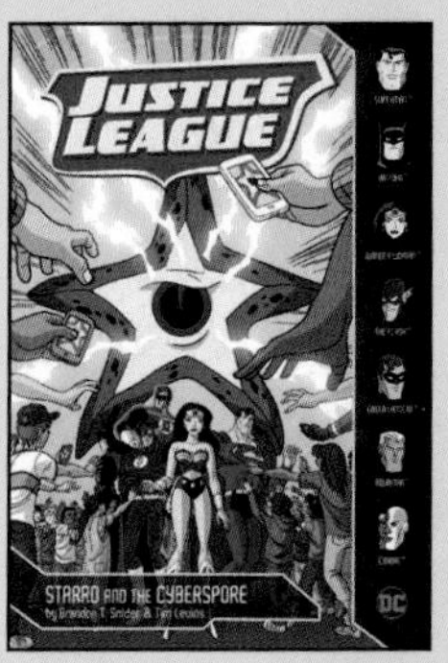
JUSTICE LEAGUE
STARRO AND THE CYBERSPORE
by Brandon T. Snider & Tim Levins
DC

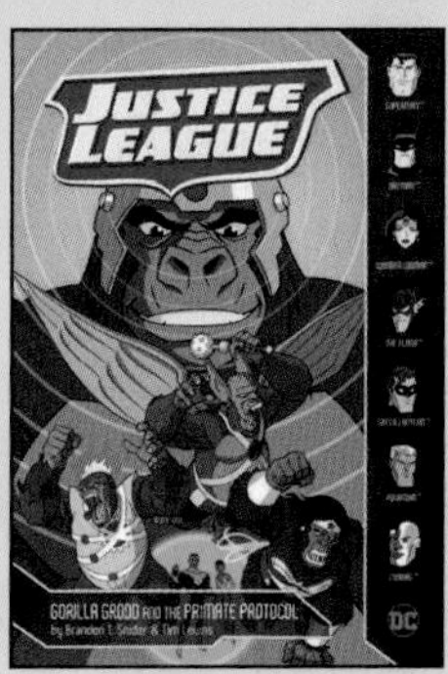
JUSTICE LEAGUE
GORILLA GRODD AND THE PRIMATE PROTOCOL
by Brandon T. Snider & Tim Levins
DC

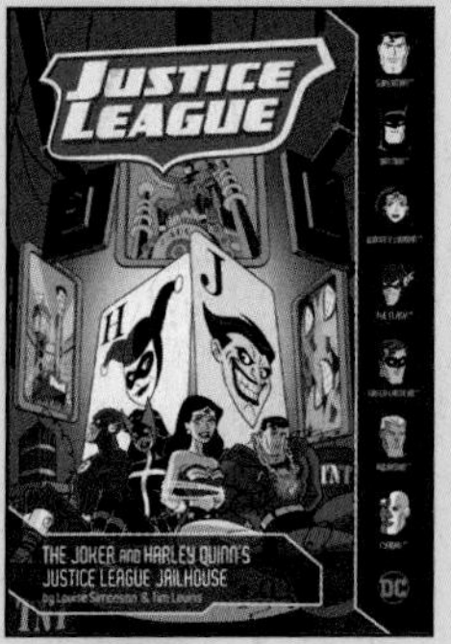
JUSTICE LEAGUE
THE JOKER AND HARLEY QUINN'S JUSTICE LEAGUE JAILHOUSE
by Louise Simonson & Tim Levins
DC

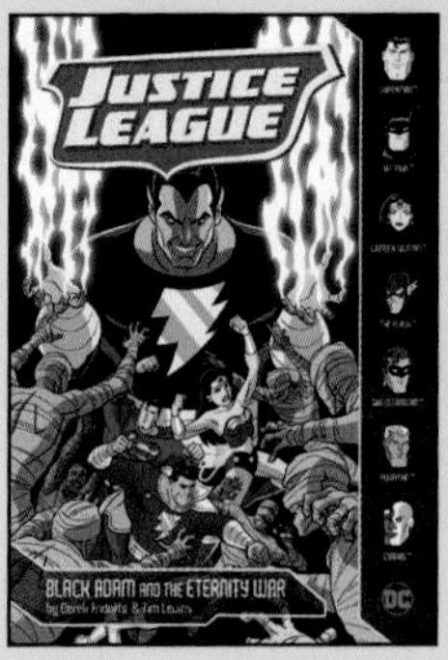
JUSTICE LEAGUE
BLACK ADAM AND THE ETERNITY WAR
by Derek Fridolfs & Tim Levins
DC

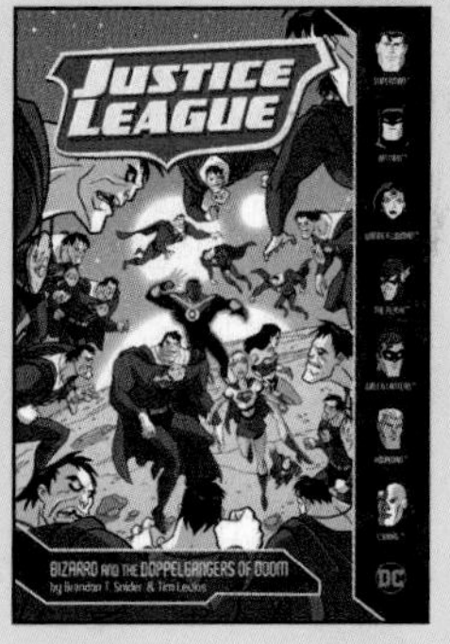
JUSTICE LEAGUE
BIZARRO AND THE DOPPELGANGERS OF DOOM
by Brandon T. Snider & Tim Levins
DC

ONLY FROM capstone

GLOSSARY

blueprint (BLOO-print)—a plan for a building

camouflage (KA-muh-flahzh)—coloring or covering that makes something look like its surroundings

communicator (kuh-MYOO-nuh-kay-tor)—a device used to talk to someone over a long distance

diabolical (dye-uh-BOL-ik-uhl)—extremely wicked

instinct (IN-stingkt)—behavior that is natural rather than learned

invulnerable (in-VUHL-nur-uh-buhl)—unable to be harmed

paralyze (PAY-ruh-lize)—to cause a loss of the ability to control the muscles

psychiatrist (sye-KYE-uh-trist)—a medical doctor who is trained to treat emotional and mental illness

satellite (SAT-uh-lite)—a spacecraft that circles Earth

scheme (SKEEM)—a plan or plot for doing something

shackles (SHAK-uhlz)—a pair of metal rings locked around the wrists or ankles of a prisoner

telescopic (tel-uh-SKOP-ik)—able to see or magnify distant objects

THINK

1. Superman goes after the Joker and Harley Quinn on his own. Why do you think he does that? What should he have done instead?

2. Lex Luthor supplies the Joker and Harley with many of their weapons. Could they have captured the Justice League without them? Why or why not?

3. Green Lantern creates duplicates of the heroes to save them from the Joker's trap. How else could he, Cyborg, or Batman have freed them safely?

WRITE

1. The Joker uses video clips of his crimes to make his captives laugh. Make a list of TV shows you would play to keep someone laughing.

2. The Joker and Harley Quinn argue about whether Superman or Wonder Woman is more powerful. Write a paragraph about which hero you think is more powerful and why.

3. Superman captures Lex Luthor at the end of the story. Write a short scene that shows what happens after he grabs Lex's shoulder.

AUTHOR

LOUISE SIMONSON enjoys writing about monsters, science fiction, fantasy characters, and super heroes. She has authored the award-winning Power Pack series, several best-selling X-Men titles, the Web of Spider-Man series for Marvel Comics, and the Superman: Man of Steel series for DC Comics. She has also written many books for kids. Louise is married to comic artist and writer Walter Simonson and lives in the suburbs of New York City.

ILLUSTRATOR

TIM LEVINS is best known for his work on the Eisner Award-winning DC Comics series Batman: Gotham Adventures. Tim has illustrated other DC titles, such as *Justice League Adventures*, *Batgirl*, *Metal Men*, and *Scooby-Doo*, and has also done work for Marvel Comics and Archie Comics. Tim enjoys life in Midland, Ontario, Canada, with his wife, son, dog, and two horses.

GLOSSARY

channel (CHA-nuhl)—to convey or direct one thing into another

hologram (HOL-uh-gram)—an image made by laser beams that looks three-dimensional

insecurity (in-si-KYOOR-i-tee)—a personal characteristic that someone feels anxious or unsure about

instinct (IN-stingkt)—behavior that is natural rather than learned

manipulate (muh-NIP-yuh-late)—to change something in a clever way to influence people to do what you want

molecule (MOL-uh-kyool)—the atoms making up the smallest unit of a substance

stealth (STELTH)—the ability to move secretly

transform (transs-FORM)—to make a great change in something

transmute (transs-MYOOT)—to change the form, appearance, or nature of something

telepathic (te-leh-PATH-ik)—able to communicate from one mind to another without speech or signs

teleport (TELL-uh-port)—to transport oneself by instantly disappearing from one place and reappearing in another

STRENGTH IN NUMBERS

ONLY FROM capstone

HANUKKAH

by
Cathy Goldberg Fishman

illustrations by
Mary O'Keefe Young

On My Own

HOLIDAYS

Carolrhoda Books, Inc./Minneapolis

For the patient ears of Laurie, Sherri, Elise, and Nancy — C. G. F.

For my loved ones: Peree, Brendan, Myles, Dana, and Maggie — M. O'K. Y

Special thanks to Rabbi Jordan Parr for his help with the preparation of this book.

Publisher's Note: The land in which the Hanukkah story takes place is sometimes referred to as Judah but is more commonly known as Judea. We have chosen to use the more common name for the region.

Text copyright © 2004 by Cathy Goldberg Fishman
Illustrations copyright © 2004 by Mary O'Keefe Young

This book is available in two editions:
Library binding by Carolrhoda Books, Inc., a division of Lerner Publishing Group
Soft cover by First Avenue Editions, an imprint of Lerner Publishing Group
241 First Avenue North
Minneapolis, MN 55401 U.S.A.

Website address: www.lernerbooks.com

Library of Congress Cataloging-in-Publication Data

Fishman, Cathy Goldberg.
　　Hanukkah / by Cathy Goldberg Fishman ; illustrations by Mary O'Keefe Young.
　　　　p.　cm. — (On my own holidays)
　　Summary: Introduces the Jewish Festival of Lights, or Hanukkah, relating the story behind the holiday and how it is celebrated.
　　ISBN: 1–57505–195–8 (lib. bdg. : alk. paper)
　　1. Hanukkah—Juvenile literature. [1. Hanukkah. 2. Holidays.] I. Young, Mary O'Keefe, ill. II. Title. III. Series.
BM695.H3 F58 2004
296.4'35—dc21   2002006814

Manufactured in the United States of America
1　2　3　4　5　6　–　JR　–　09　08　07　06　05　04